POKéMON®

EYE SEE IT!
CAN YOU FIND THEM ALL?

By Maria Barbo
Illustrated by Josie Yee

ISBN 978-0-545-09939-4

© 2010 Pokémon. ©1995-2010 Nintendo/Creatures Inc./GAME FREAK inc. TM and ® and character names are trademarks of Nintendo.
Published by Scholastic Inc.
SCHOLASTIC and associated logos are trademarks and/or registered trademarks of Scholastic Inc.

12 11 10 9 8 7 6 5 4 3 2 1   10 11 12 13 14 15/0

Designed by Cheung Tai
Printed in the U.S.A.   56
First printing, June 2010
Scholastic Inc.

New York   Toronto   London   Auckland
Sydney   Mexico City   New Delhi   Hong Kong

Are you ready to start your adventure in Johto? Kids can become Pokémon Trainers after their tenth birthdays. Each new Trainer picks up his first Poké Ball from Professor Elm and sets out to earn Gym Badges, compete against other Pokémon Trainers, and find Pokémon they've never seen before. So head out to Johto and pick up your first Pokémon — Chikorita, Cyndaquil, or Totodile!

Can you find all the objects and Pokémon hiding in this picture?

Sneaker   Cap   Spinarak   Poké Ball

Politoed Ledyba Sudowoodo

Bonus
question:

There are 3 Natu
hiding in this
picture. Can you
spot them?

Pokémon on the loose! Everything is topsy-turvy in this Pokémon lab. Looks like Chikorita, Cyndaquil, and Totodile had a great time making a massive mess! Or was this the work of Team Rocket? No time to figure it out — the new Pokémon Trainers are on their way. The professor has to clean up this lab faster than you can say, "Pika, Pika, Pikachu!"

Can you find them all?

Microscope Elekid Porygon2 Mineral Badge

Bonus:
How many different kinds of Poké Balls can you find hidden in this picture?

Pecha Berry   Test Tube   Friend Ball

Prepare for trouble. Make it double! Team Rocket is at it again. This time, Jessie, James, and Meowth have set up a not-so-clever scheme to nab a net full of Azumarill. Let's hope our heroes arrive in time to rescue this pack of Water-type Pokémon.

Can you find them all?

Hive Badge

Nest Ball

Tamato Berry

Sunkern

Slowking

Aipom

Jumpluff

Bonus:
How many Azumarill did Team Rocket try to steal?

Dawn, Ash, and Brock are enjoying a night at the carnival. There are balloons, cotton candy, and a giant Ferris wheel! What could be more fun? Now, if only the three Trainers could figure out where Happiny has wandered off to . . .

Can you find them all?

Net Ball

Happiny

Pichu

Ash's Pokédex

Bonus:

Count the Cleffa! How many did you find?

Igglybuff

Jessie

James

Make a splash! Like many Pokémon Trainers, Ash, Dawn, and Brock can't resist a day at the beach. It's time for some fun in the sun — and time to check out the many amazing Water-type Pokémon. Some incredible moves are on display down by the seashore!

Can you find them all?

Kingdra   **Dawn's Pokédex**   **Wooper**   **Fog Badge**

Quagsire

Marill

Qwilfish

Bonus:

How many different Water-type Pokémon can you count in this picture?

Welcome to the arena! Major competitions like Johto's Silver League Conference are held in arenas like this one. There's a big crowd for today's Trainer battle. The first Trainer sent out Charizard, and the second Trainer sent out Scizor! Charizard is a Fire-and-Flying-type Pokémon known for taking down opponents with its powerful Flamethrower attack. It's a mega match-up! Who will win?

Can you find them all?

Murkrow   Repeat Ball   Smeargle   Xatu

Togepi

Granbull

Zephyr Badge

Bonus:

Based on type, who is most likely to win this battle?

Mountain mayhem! A field full of Mareep and Flaaffy are in deep trouble! These fluffy Electric-types store electricity in their woolly coats, but they avoid battles . . . if they can! Houndour has its eye on a pile of Berries the flock has collected. Is Ampharos's ThunderShock attack powerful enough to protect the Berries from a hungry Houndour?

Can you find them all?

Glacier Badge

Miltank

Larvitar

Pineco

Skiploom

Delibird

Sitrus Berry

Bonus:

How many Mareep and Flaaffy can you count? Don't fall asleep!

Playtime on the playground! The Pokémon here are enjoying some fun in the sun during a relaxing day at the park. Sometimes Phanpy bumps its friends with its snout — like a big hug. But those playful Pokémon better be alert — Team Rocket is hiding nearby!

Can you find them all?

Sentret

Togetic

Granbull

Espeon

Hitmontop

Magby

Smoochum

Bonus:

Can you find Team Rocket hiding in this picture?

BOO! Teddiursa got lost on his hunt for honey. Now the Little Bear Pokémon is alone in a spooky forest. There are lots of Pokémon hiding in the trees and nearby cave, and a Misdreavus is looking for someone to play a prank on. How long can Teddiursa hide from this mischievous Ghost-type Pokémon? Maybe Noctowl can show Teddiursa the way home!

Can you find them all?

Forretress   Swinub   Rising Badge   Heracross

Bonus:

How many Dark-type Pokémon can you find?

lack Apricorn   Houndoom   Oran Berry

How many did you find?

The bonus items are circled in black.

pp. 4-5

pp. 6-7

BONUS ANSWER:
There are seven different Poké Balls.

pp. 8-9

BONUS ANSWER:
Team Rocket tried to steal eight Azumarill.

pp. 10-11

BONUS ANSWER:
There are five Cleffa.

pp. 12-13

BONUS ANSWER:
There are seventeen different Water-type Pokémon.